MW00526344

I LOVE YOU
Grandma

Autumn
Publishing

Published in 2020
by Autumn Publishing
Cottage Farm
Sywell
NN6 0BJ
www.igloobooks.com

Copyright © 2018 Autumn Publishing
Autumn is an imprint of Bonnier Books UK

All rights reserved. No part of this publication may be
reproduced or transmitted in any form or by any means,
electronic, or mechanical, including photocopying, recording,
or by any information storage and retrieval system,
without permission in writing from the publisher.

0220 001
2 4 6 8 10 9 7 5 3 1
ISBN 978-1-83903-861-7

Illustrated by Lizzie Walkley
Written by Melanie Joyce

Cover designed by Nicholas Gage
Interiors designed by Alice Dainty
Edited by Jasmin Peppiatt

Printed and manufactured in China

I LOVE YOU
Grandma

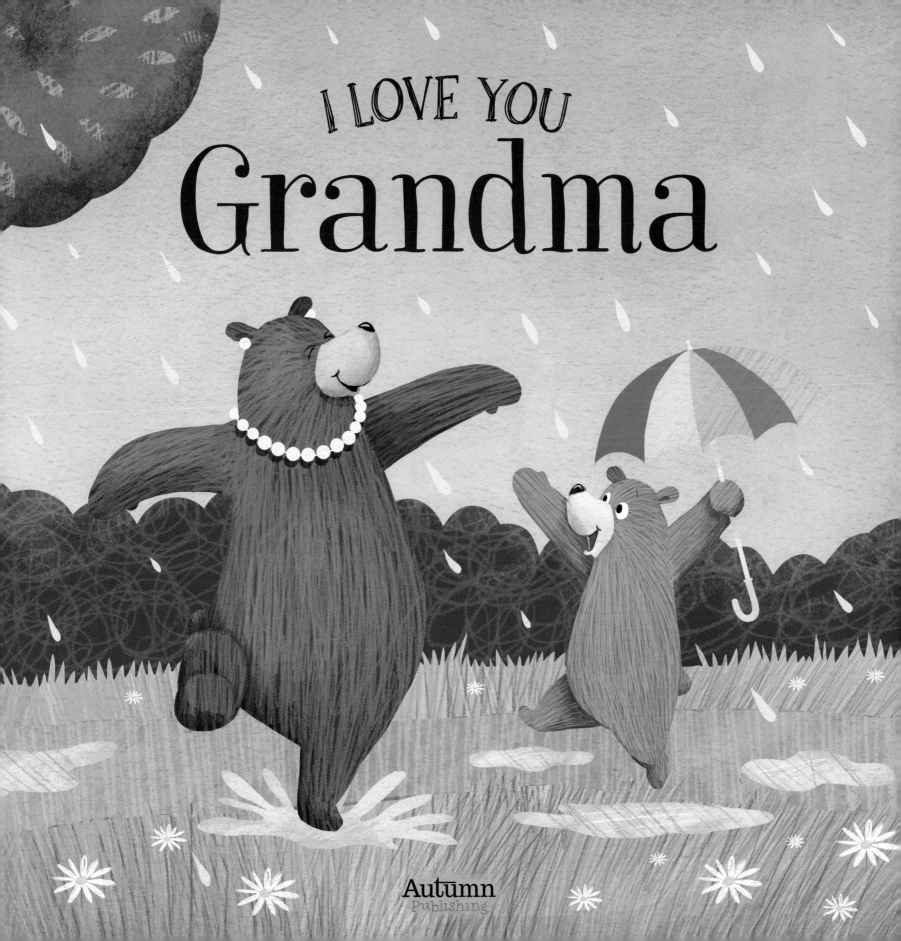

Autumn
Publishing

I love you, Grandma,

because when you see me...

... you scoop me up gently
and hold me tenderly.

You **kiss** me...

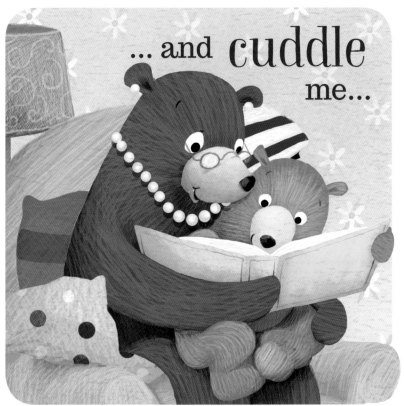

... and **cuddle** me...

... **again** and **again**...

... and you smell like fresh meadow flowers after the rain.

I really love playtime
when I stay with you.

We play catch...

... and chase...

... and hide-and-seek too.

I love you because...

... you are always SO kind.

If I make a mistake, you say,

If I'm worried or scared, you say,

Everyone cries.

We lay in the grass
and gaze up at the sky...

I love you because we have fun all day...

... and there's always five more minutes to play.

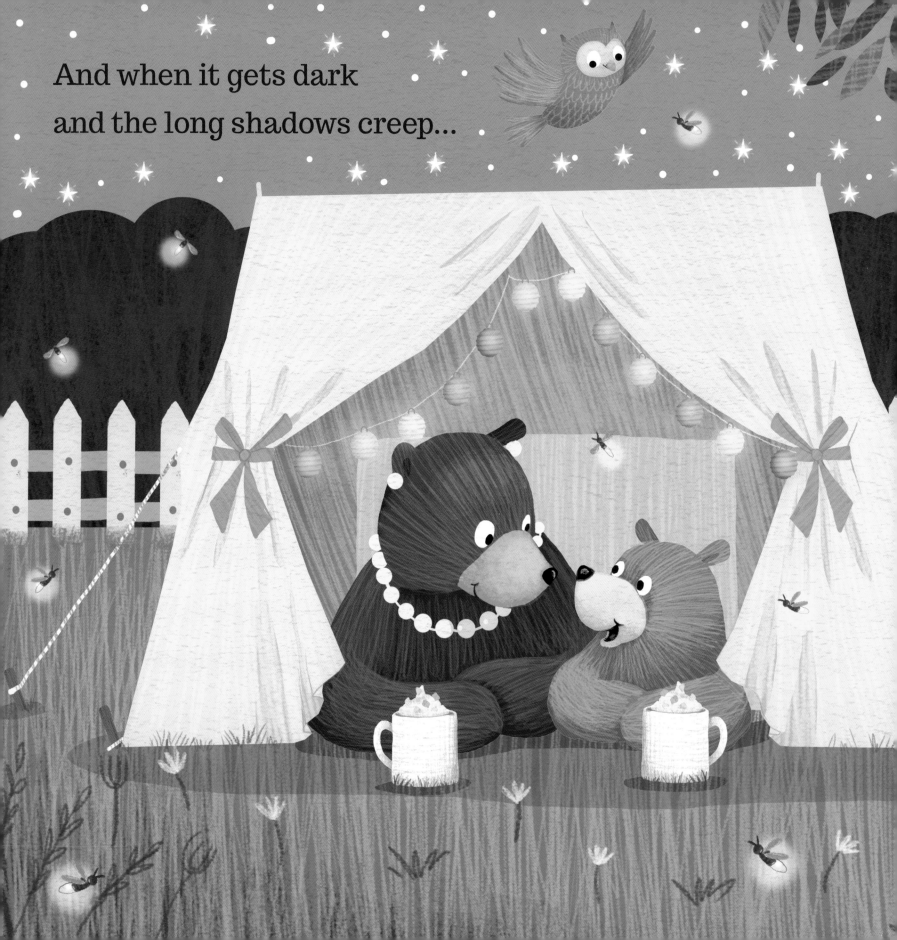

And when it gets dark
and the long shadows creep...

... we gaze at the stars
before I go to sleep.

Grandma, you always make everything seem right. And I feel so safe as I snuggle down at night.

I love you, Grandma, I really, truly do.

There will never be anyone as special as you.